THE PRINCESS OF ÉLEVÉ

MONTOBA

A FULL LENGTH PLAY

AN HISTORICAL FANTASY

By

ED STRUM

Semi-Finalist - 2007 Stanley Drama Awards

THE PRINCESS

OF

ÉLEVÉ

Books by Ed Strum

THE CONNOISSSEURS – A Play

MONTOBA – A Novel

THE BURROW – A Play

JOURNEY OF THE SCROLLS – A Novel

JOURNEY OF THE SCROLLS – SPECIAL EDITION

THE PRINCESS OF ÉLEVÉ – A Play

EVERY DAY IS A GOOD DAY – A Play

THE HOLLOW PENCIL – A Play

CASCADIA and THE GREAT PANDEMIC – A Novel

ADAM'S ARK & THE GREAT PANDEMIC – A Play

RICHIE – A Poetic Play in One Scene

A SENSORY FEAST – An Anthology of Prose Poetry

SYNOPSIS

In the year 2037, two friends and fellow science students, Archie and Yuri, have each made interesting discoveries. Archie's interest in archaeology led her to join a team of international archaeologists in Southeast Asia where she uncovered ancient tablets near the site of the last known eruption of a super volcano. Yuri's interest in astronomy, meanwhile, has led him to discover a strange object in space, about which he's just presented a paper. He's been tracking this object, which is headed for earth and which has been exhibiting unusual behavior.

While deciphering the tablets, Archie finds hidden in the "pages" strange magic "wafers" alluded to in the text. These magical wafers, the writings tell her, will transport her back in time. Radiocarbon dating tests indicate that the tablets are about 75000 years old. Yuri is sure it's a joke someone is playing on them, says it can't be true, and that it must be a hoax. Before Archie can stop him, he grabs one of the wafers, pops it into his mouth, and disappears. Archie is stunned but soon decides to do the same.

They are catapulted back to the ancient city of Montoba. There they discover evidence of amazing technical advances, but also terrible dangers, including war, strange creatures and environmental hazards. Many living creatures, including humans, have been pushed to the brink of extinction.

They become part of a small party, which includes an ancient leprechaun, a gnome, a fairy, elves and a wizard. It is their mission to rescue the "lady" who is the last remaining princess of Montoba, and one of the few humans remaining on earth. They must solve a difficult riddle, find a hidden treasure, protect the secrets of this ancient world, and help the princess achieve her destiny.

On their journey, they are followed by a hooded figure, who is accompanied by a small misshapen goblin. They're attacked by terrifying creatures, but also encounter friendly ones that save them and help them on their journey. As they proceed, the rumbling and shaking of the ground becomes increasingly more ominous. The success or failure of their quest affects the destiny of all mankind.

This humorous fantasy adventure play touches adult issues of a cultural, environmental, political and social nature, as well as various fields of study including archaeology, anthropology, biology, chemistry, evolution, genetics, geology, and physics.

THE PRINCESS OF ÉLEVÉ

CAST OF CHARACTERS
(In order of appearance)

Archie – 17, born in 2020. Female.
An archaeology student.

Yuri – 19, born in 2018. Male. Russian.
An astronomy student. Speaks with Russian accent.

Narrator – M or F.

Pre – age unknown. M (or F).
A leprechaun. An elf who reveals hidden treasure if caught.

Murgi – M or F.
A gnome. Dwarfish creature living under ground. Guards precious treasure hoard.

Scarth – M or F.
An evil, hooded figure. Powerful enemy of all. Has magical powers. Intent on stealing all the treasures and technical advances of the ancient world of Montoba. Leader of the Dungé tribe.

Igor – M or F.
A misshapen goblin with a dual personality. Companion to Scarth. Seeks treasure.

Calypso – Female.
A fairy. Small, mischievous creature in human form, clever, having magical powers.

WOOWON and WOOTU - TWO WOOs – M or F.
Elves. Small, mischievous creatures, clever, having magical powers. Speak in rhyme.

Mia – age 19. Female.
A beautiful, gentle and intelligent princess. Leader of the Élevé tribe.

Screaming Meemies - M or F (4 or more).
A group of hideous small screaming nerve-wracking ragged creatures.

Tenty - Giant Caterpillar – M or F (several people).
A large shy multi-legged creature. Gentle in nature, timid and afraid.

Saber-Toothed Tiger – M or F (2 people).
A large vicious prehistoric creature that attacks and eats anything.

Shrooms – M or F (4 or more).
Small poisonous, walking, talking, winged, ugly creatures that look like mushrooms.

Sam – age unknown. M (or F).
A wizard.

Flying Unicorn Crab – M or F (3 people).
A large crablike creature with long legs, giant claws, four large wings and a hornlike projection in the center that can render a victim unconscious.

Horned Draken – M or F (Several).
A huge sea monster from prehistoric times, ancestor of many recent monsters. Roams the inland sea, roars loudly, has large bulging eyes and nostrils, horns sticking up at the end of its nose, large mouth and teeth, a long tongue and eight arms. It breathes fire, has hard scaly triangular projections on its back, connected by webbing and loves to eat people.

Fins – M or F (4 or more).
Small versions of modern day dolphins.

Gryphon – M or F (2 people).
A flying horse/lion with a head of a condor or eagle. The hind legs and hooves are of a horse and the front legs and paws with sharp claws or talons are like those of a lion or bird of prey. The head is that of a condor or large eagle with a very big sharp hooked beak. Fortunately, this is a friendly beast and loyal to those in the group.

Rolly – M or F.
A troll. A creature sometimes friendly and sometimes mischievous, dwarfish or gigantic, that lives in caves or under bridges.

Giant Troll – M or F.
A huge troll that carries a large club. Attacks all that come near. Very slow in movement.

Giant Cabbage Skunk – M or F.
A talking, walking large stinky creature that is the ancient ancestor of both the skunk cabbage and the common skunk. It is very large, has black and white stripes all over its body and legs, except for its head, which is bright yellow, similar to the new growth of the skunk cabbage. It has an overwhelming stench. It stinks so strongly that the largest of creatures cannot stand its smell.

Walking Ivy – M or F.
A walking plant with large tendrils that ensnare and strangle victims. Slow to move. It is carnivorous, lives below ground, and has evolved from an ivy plant that found its habitat above ground destroyed.

Two-Headed Gorgon – M or F (2 people).
A two-headed creature with snakes for hair and eyes that turn beholders to stone.

Flying Furies – M or F (4 or more)
Ferocious winged creatures resembling a cross between a bat, bee and bug.

Giant Moth – M or F (1 to 3).
A winged creature resembling our moth (originally Tenty the caterpillar).

Prince Peter – age 21. Male.
A handsome prince that had disappeared – the leader of the Midé tribe.

Flying Beetle – M or F (2 people).
A spaceship that is alive and looks like a huge flying beetle.

Cast and Set Summary

Cast size: Minimum 10, Optimum (15-30), Maximum 60 or more. The cast of this play can **and should** include those of any age, ethnicity, or gender, although the characters of Archie, Yuri, the Princess and the Prince would be best at the appropriate gender.

Set: The play is designed to utilize a simple set with minor changes from scene to scene. The play emphasizes action as well as fast dialogue. The set can be a blank stage with suggestions of the different environments or can be more elaborate. This play has been staged and rehearsed with a large cast of high school and middle school students (see Appendices B and C for suggested staging). The same is true with respect to costumes where imaginative minimal suggestions of characters can be used. The practical minimum cast size is 12 (see Appendix G). There are 10 major speaking roles and several other minor speaking roles (see Appendix E.)

If you are staging a production of this play, and wish staging production suggestions, please contact the author.

Scene Summary

The action takes place in 2037, and in very ancient times, in a series of underground caves and caverns connected by passageways, on a huge lake, and above ground on a devastated landscape.

Prologue: January, 2037; Tablets; magic wafers, an object in space

ACT I: 75000 years ago; SE Asia; days or weeks between scenes
    Scene One: In the cavern of the leprechaun
    Scene Two: The Two Woos and the mirror
    Scene Three: Screaming Meemies and Tenty
    Scene Four: Shroom Attack

ACT II: some time later – days or weeks between each scene
    Scene One: Archie and Montoba
    Scene Two: Draken and Fins
    Scene Three: The Round-Up
    Scene Four: The Troll and the Flying Crab
    Scene Five: Giant Troll, Cabbage Skunk and Walking Ivy

ACT III: even later – days or weeks between each scene
    Scene One: The Princess and the Gorgon
    Scene Two: Flying Furies and the Gryphon
    Scene Three: Saving the Princess
    Scene Four: The Flying Beetle and the Treasure

Epilogue: Year 2037 – few weeks after prologue; an object in space

Running Time: Approximately 75 Minutes with rapid set changes

Appendices
Appendix A: Costume Design / Costumes
Appendix B: Set Design, Pieces and Effects
Appendix C: Prop Design / Prop List
Appendix D: Special Effects, Sound Effects and Music
Appendix E: Characters by Scene Matrix
Appendix F: The Pirate Chief's Riddle
Appendix G: Actors and Characters Matrix

THE PRINCESS OF ÉLEVÉ

PROLOGUE: A student room. Two chairs, a small table, and a lamp. Archie looks at thin slate like sheets using a magnifying glass. They are dusty and old. She looks at four gray wafers on the table and makes notes. Yuri enters, puts backpack down. They hug each other.

ARCHIE
Yuri! I've missed you. How'd the presentation go?

YURI
(They sit.) Not so hot! Science professors aren't as open-minded as you think when their beliefs are challenged. *(Pause.)* How's it coming on the tablets, Archie? Finished yet?

ARCHIE
(Excited.) Almost! I've figured out most of the characters. I'll show you. Look! *(Points to notebook.)* I deciphered the language. It's based on sounds, like our phonemes.

YURI
Makes sense. Ancient languages were passed on by speaking. So why is it written down?

ARCHIE
To pass on a description of their world! Whoever wrote these invented this language just for that purpose.

YURI
How do you know what the characters mean?

ARCHIE
That's the neat thing about these tablets. The writer has added little pictures of objects as he goes. Like the Mayan's rebus. He wants us to understand what the markings mean.

YURI
Did you find out yet how old the tablets are?

ARCHIE

The radiocarbon dating test arrives today. There's something strange, Yuri. The writing changes part way through, as if another person took over the writing. The first writer tells of the technology of this civilization. Read this! My translation! *(He reads).*

NARRATOR

"There once was a great city called Montoba. The city surrounded a huge mountain, and towered one kilometer into the air. Tunnels and caverns extended the city ten kilometers below the surface. It got its energy from solar energy collecting sunlight and concentrating it into the city. It also received heat from boiling thermal fountains and rivers and from the proximity of the superheated magma chamber."

ARCHIE

One kilometer high! Astounding! Yuri, remember that Japanese skyscraper project? They planned a building a mile high. They never built it, did they? But in ancient times they did!

YURI

Come on! An ancient, advanced civilization? Get real!

ARCHIE

Well, it's possible! Look at how advanced the civilization was in Egypt, and Greece, and Rome! We still can't duplicate Egyptian technology. Like their mummification!

YURI

Yes, but we've known about these civilizations for some time, and they existed a few thousand years ago. You think this is much older?

ARCHIE

Read on! There's more! It's the second writer now. *(He reads.)*

NARRATOR

"Now the city's in ruins. The wars between the three tribes destroyed the city. The people were threatened by wild creatures, strange killer clouds, and the towering mountain. The dangers have pushed most living creatures to the brink of extinction."

YURI

(He jumps up.) Archie! A civilization that we didn't know existed? That became extinct?

ARCHIE

(Sulking) Well, it's possible! You don't believe me?

YURI

Be realistic! Someone's playing a hoax on you! What about those wafers hidden in the tablets? You really believe what the text says?

ARCHIE

What? *(She holds up the wafers.)* You mean that these could transport you back in time?

YURI

Yes!

ARCHIE

Well, maybe! *(Subdued.)* Yuri, I need to go back to where I found the tablets. I've got to know why this was written, who wrote it, why they constantly mention the mountain, and I need to solve the riddle!

YURI

Riddle? What riddle?

ARCHIE

The tablets contain a riddle referring to a hidden treasure. It's kind of vague. I'm sure it's obscure on purpose.

YURI

Don't you think you're getting carried away? Riddle? Treasure?

ARCHIE

No more than you! Aren't you imagining this meteor you're tracking is jumping around? *(Pause.)* I'm sorry!

YURI

No, I'm not imagining it! Look! *(Gets photos.)* These time lapse photos show that it changes direction. It's behaving very erratically.

3

ARCHIE

That's not possible!

YURI

You? A scientist? Telling me it's not possible?

ARCHIE

It must be gravitational pull from nearby objects. How else would you explain it?

YURI

All I know is that it's headed here and getting closer – and appears to be honing in on us!

ARCHIE

You really think some space object is headed here? How big is it? When will it get here?

YURI

I'll know in a few weeks. I'd like to join you, but I really should stay here, since it's my discovery!

ARCHIE

I promise I'll be back in less than three weeks! *(A knock. Archie takes a letter from a courier, reads it to herself. Yuri reads it.)*

YURI

75,000 years old! Unbelievable! *(Silence.)* Archie, if it's true and not a hoax, then explain this to me - how did these tablets last so long?

ARCHIE

They're made of a hard slate like substance. The markings were made with a diamond point. Like that material invented a few years ago. Thin, strong, light, same molecular structure as coal and diamonds. Carbon nanotubes! Remember? 10 times lighter than steel and 100 times stronger! They were going to build a space elevator!

YURI

They never did! How did the writings survive without being worn?

ARCHIE

Don't forget they've been buried all this time, and not exposed to air. Yuri, do you realize there were intelligent people 75,000 years ago?

YURI

Yeh, sure! Wearing animal skins! Eating only meat. Barely surviving! But intelligent?

ARCHIE

Think! Remember the studies of mitochondrial DNA? Man was close to extinction 75000 years ago from a cataclysmic event, a super volcano. There may've been only a few dozen women to reproduce. All mankind's descended from them. Seven billion and all related, one big family! Isn't it possible this civilization surpassed our own by far? Then it was lost? What could've happened?

YURI

Archie, this is nonsense! It must be a hoax! I'll show you. *(He grabs a wafer from the table and pops it into his mouth. There is a boom, smoke, and he disappears. Archie picks up a wafer, looks at it and looks around for Yuri, as if to figure out what happened.)*

ARCHIE

Oh, Yuri, what have you done! *(She puts two of the wafers in the pocket of her backpack. She notices Yuri's backpack and picks it up. Softly.)* You may need this! *(Then she takes a deep breath, closes her eyes, and pops the remaining wafer into her mouth. There's a boom, smoke, and she also disappears. Darkness. Lights out.)*

End of prologue.

ACT ONE

Scene One: Archie stands in a large cavern. There's a large rock in the back of the cavern. Behind it are doodles on the wall. There are four exits from this cavern, one of which appears to be a cave with little evidence of traffic. A passageway with boulders in front and another with pebbles both lead to a third with a crumbling statue of a King in front. Yuri runs in from it.

YURI
Archie! I thought I'd blown it this time! I wasn't sure if you'd come!

ARCHIE
I couldn't let you do this alone. *(Hugs him.)* It's my mission, my journey to take. *(She points to the King.)* Where's that go?

YURI
It must be a main passageway. The others have paths to it. *(Points to worn tracks.)* Do you really think we went back 75000 years?

ARCHIE
Look around! What do you think? *(She sees the doodles.)* See! The same writings as my tablet! *(They hear a snore from under the rock.)*

YURI
Look here! What's this? *(A leprechaun, clad in green short pants, dusty jacket, and boots, wakes up, and runs off into the King tunnel.)*

ARCHIE
It's a leprechaun, Yuri!

YURI
Do your notes say anything about a leprechaun?

ARCHIE
No, but that's what it looks like.

YURI
Shall I catch it? You know the legend – a leprechaun is bound to reveal the location of its treasure!

6

ARCHIE

Leave it alone! *(Takes his arm.)* Look at these figures and doodles!

YURI

What do they say?

ARCHIE

(Peers at wall.) There's an evil looking figure I hadn't seen before. Maybe he's after the treasure.

YURI

Treasure? Evil figure? I can't believe it! You're such a romantic!

ARCHIE

What's this? Looks like a beetle! Connected to this treasure?

YURI

Beetles? Hmmm! *(Moves to King.)* Look, I don't want it to escape!

ARCHIE

All right, but be gentle! It seemed so terrified.

YURI

Don't worry! I have a very gentle touch! *(She smiles. Yuri exits.)*

ARCHIE

Don't be long! We don't know what wild creatures are around. Let's see! *(She looks at the engravings. Yuri returns with the leprechaun.)*

PRE

Ontde urtha ema! Ee ontwa unra ayawa! *(He shrinks to floor.)*

ARCHIE

What's he saying?

YURI

How should I know? Sounds like gibberish to me.

PRE

Aaaah! (*A sound of recognition.*) Oh, you've finally come! I said "Don't hurt me! I won't run away!"

ARCHIE

You're a leprechaun? And you speak our language?

PRE

Yes, and yes! I speak all languages.

YURI

You have a name, Mr. Leprechaun? How long have you been there?

PRE

My name is Pre. How long? Hmmm, well, that depends. Let's just say quite a long time.

YURI

(To Archie.) He speaks in riddles!

ARCHIE

I'll talk to him! *(She pushes Yuri to the cave.)* Check out that cave. I'll ask him about the engravings. *(He exits. To Pre.)* What did you mean, "You've finally come"?

PRE

I knew someone would find the tablets one day and come to help us.

ARCHIE

Help? With what?

PRE

The quest! The search! I can't do it by myself.

ARCHIE

Yuri says you're bound to tell us where the treasure is. Is that true?

PRE

I can't tell you, but I can show you! I must warn you that it'll be a dangerous journey.

8

ARCHIE

Dangerous?

PRE

My lady, there're still some terrifying creatures left in our world. Besides, I could never take this long journey alone. Our legend says someday you'd come and help us. I've been waiting so long! *(The ground shakes and rumbles.)* We must go! There's no time to lose!

ARCHIE

It's only a small earthquake.

PRE

I know, but it'll get worse! We still have time.

ARCHIE

We've got to wait for Yuri! Where are we? What is this place?

PRE

You're in the great city called Montoba! Or what remains of it. It runs several hundred kilometers from end to end. It's been destroyed by the wars and the fiery mountain.

ARCHIE

Destroyed? How? What "wars"?

PRE

The tribe from the lower ground – the Dungé we call them – tried to conquer the world. The other tribes – the Midé and the Élevé – banded together to save themselves.

ARCHIE

Who won?

PRE

What?

ARCHIE

The war! Who won the war?

PRE

No one really wins wars. Almost everyone was killed. It was awful!

ARCHIE

I'm sorry. I'm confused! Which tribe are you from?

PRE

The Midé! There're not many of us left!

ARCHIE

Then the Élevé were your allies. Are there many of them?

PRE

No. But the most important one of them may be. Their leader!

ARCHIE

Who's that?

PRE

The Princess! She's missing. We don't know what happened to her.

ARCHIE

You said something about the mountain? What about it?

PRE

Legend says the mountain blew up long ago and eventually became a huge deep lake, but we still call it the mountain. Everyone's afraid of it. They think a terrible vengeful god lives there. Now and then a strange cloud comes from the lake and kills everyone nearby.

ARCHIE

A cloud? (*Pause)* How do they die? From suffocation?

PRE

No one knows! It just rolls across the land killing everything for miles!

ARCHIE

I think I know what it is! Carbon 13!

10

PRE

What's that?

ARCHIE

Comes from underground and generates a thick cloud of CO_2.
We've some killer lakes…

PRE

(*Strong rumbling and shaking. He moves to tunnel.*) Let's go! It's a
long journey!

ARCHIE

Wait! Yuri'll be back soon. (*She is persistent and presses on.*) Did
you write the tablets?

PRE

Some of them. Where is he? We must go! We don't have much time!

ARCHIE

Why are you so worried? Much time for what?

PRE

(*Hesitant.*) It's the mountain. It's getting worse! (*Sounds from cave.*)

ARCHIE

It's Yuri. What do these drawings mean? Did you carve them?

PRE

Some of them! (*Pre acts nervously and shows he wants to leave.*)
They tell about the wars we fought – and the terrible mountain.

ARCHIE

What's this? It looks like a beetle? (*At this point Yuri returns,
holding a gnome by the hand, and holding an axe in his other hand.
The gnome is dragging a large sack.*)

YURI

Look what I found! Some sort of dwarf!

PRE

He's a gnome. (*He talks to gnome.*) Reaye ouye koye?

MURGI

Ye asweye raidafye utbeye eheye iddeye otneye urtheye emeye.

PRE

Troduceinye ourelfseye!

MURGI

Oh, hello! My name's Murgi!

PRE

He's a friend. He wants to go with us.

YURI

(*Gives him back his axe.*) What's in your sack?

MURGI

Presents! These're for you. You'll need them on our quest. (*He pulls out two rapiers.*)

PRE

(*He holds one.*) They're made from the same material as the tablet sheets. Very light, strong, and very sharp. With diamond points. Here! (*He hands Yuri the rapier.*)

MURGI

(*Hesitant – to Archie.*) Are you a female? A woman? Our women were all warriors, but I didn't think that your women were......

ARCHIE

Oh, don't worry! (*She shows she's a woman, for example by letting down her hair. She takes a rapier from him.*) I can fight as well as any man. (*She brandishes her sword and Murgi jumps back. Meanwhile, Pre pulls several orange wafers from the sack.*)

PRE

(*Suddenly remembers something. To Archie.*) Did you bring those other wafers?

ARCHIE

(She pulls them out from her knapsack.) Yes, why?

PRE

(Smiles.) Good! You'll need them some day. *(Hands each of them two orange wafers.)* Don't get these mixed up! We wouldn't want to lose you. These are to eat – for food.

ARCHIE

(She holds them in her hand, dubiously.) Food? Are you serious?

PRE

One'll last you a very long time. This is one of our secret inventions. *(Archie shrugs, puts them in her backpack. Pre pulls a recorder from the sack, thinks, then puts it back.)*

YURI

(To Murgi.) How'd you know we're going on a journey?

MURGI

I want to go with you! We must save our lady! I want to get back at..*(Pre stops him.)* Well, what I mean is, you'll need a strong arm! *(There's a noise from the tunnel with boulders. Pre grabs Archie, who grabs her backpack. They hurry toward the King tunnel.)*

PRE

Hurry! There's no time to tell you anymore. *(They exit. Yuri grabs his backpack, and the sack, and follows, with Murgi close behind.)*

There's another noise. Scarth, a hooded figure, enters followed by Igor, a misshapen goblin. Scarth carries a staff/stick and Igor carries a small walking stick.

SCARTH

Iddaz onyaz earhaz hattaz oisenaz? Eeplpaz?

IGOR

Yaz! Everalsaz oicevaz!

SCARTH

I thought I heard voices!

IGOR

Yes, Master Scarth! So did I!

SCARTH

(*Sharply.*) Don't use my name, you miserable ugly dwarf!

IGOR

Yes, master! As you say!

SCARTH

I did say! Let's get on with it! After them, you slimy toad!

IGOR

Where are they going? Why are we following them?

SCARTH

They'll lead us to the princess. Don't ask questions. Let's go! *(He strides out after the group. Igor follows.)*

A fairy comes out from the cave, hears their departing footsteps, and lets out a terrifying scream in the cavern. The fairy pulls out her wand, points it at the entrance of the passage with boulders and causes the yells and noises to come from there, periodically, as if fading. She goes back into the cave she was in. Scarth and Igor rush back in, hear the noises fading. Scarth is very angry.

SCARTH

They tricked us! They must've hid in the cave. Quickly! *(He exits after noises.)*

IGOR

Yes, master, as you wish! Stupid idiot! *(Makes faces and a bad sign. Follows slowly.)* Coming! *(Exits)*

The fairy darts out from the cave and into the King tunnel after Pre.

End of Scene One.

14

Scene Two: *A clearing in the underground passageway. Moss grows on the walls. There is another tunnel opposite their entrance and a cave entrance diagonally opposite their entry. A large rock is in the back. Pre enters, followed by Archie, Yuri, and Murgi, leans against the rock, and wipes his forehead.*

PRE
Whew, that was a long stretch! I need a rest!

YURI
Look! Another cave! I'll check it out while you rest! *(Goes to cave.)*

ARCHIE
Be careful Yuri! Pre says dangerous creatures still roam around here!

MURGI
I'll go with him, my lady! *(Hoists axe over shoulder and follows.)*

PRE
Don't take too long! We must go. I'm afraid we're being followed.

YURI
We'll be right back! *(He draws his sword.)* Whatever you are, prepare to die! *(They exit.)*

ARCHIE
Back there, Murgi mentioned saving our lady? Is that the princess?

PRE
Yes. She may be alive but we think she's in danger.

ARCHIE
Is that where we're going? Not the treasure?

PRE
She was trying to find the treasure site. We only know the general area where it's hidden.

ARCHIE
You said we're being followed? By whom?

PRE

We don't know. Perhaps our enemies. We can't take any chances.

ARCHIE

We've been traveling for days! Up and down hill, through tunnel after tunnel! It keeps getting hotter and hotter, then cool again as we climb back up. Why? Where are we?

PRE

These tunnels go several kilometers below ground. The deeper we go, the closer we get to the tunnels that go in close to the magma chamber. We get heat and energy from it.

ARCHIE

I understand. *(Pause)* How much farther do we have to go?

PRE

I'm sorry, my lady, but this's a long journey. We still have the dangerous part ahead!

ARCHIE

Why? What do you mean? What's ahead?

PRE

We have the lake to cross... *(He is stopped by Yuri and Murgi, retreating from the cave, with sword and axe raised. The two WOOs (WOOWON and WOOTU) enter. They hold black wands and advance on Yuri. WOOTU also holds a staff but does not appear to know how to use it. The TWO WOOs are the most pathetic looking elves, in complete disarray.*

YURI

You'll taste my sword! Prepare to die! *(As he backs up.)*

ARCHIE

Yuri, they look so pathetic! Don't hurt them!

WOOWON

Shall we turn them to stones?

16

WOOTU

No, let's turn them to bones!

WOOWON

Reduce them to dust?

WOOTU

We'll do what we must!

WOOWON

Let's turn them to fools!

WOOTU

Or maybe to mules!

TWOWOOs

They'll never tell
We cast a spell!

They raise their wands. The staff hangs loosely in the hand of WOOTU. Before they can cast a spell, Pre raises his staff.

PRE

Alaca wheez, doodela freeze! *(TWO WOOs freeze, wands in the air.)*

YURI

Wow! That was close! What are they?

PRE

They're called the TWO WOOs. They're probably the only elves that survived the wars. They're a bit mischievous, but generally harmless. Let's not take a chance though. Take their wands! And that staff! *(Yuri steps forward, takes the wands from their raised hands, and Murgi takes the staff.)* Alaca wheez, undothe freeze! *(They return to normal.)*

ARCHIE

They seem so forlorn and woebegone! Could they really cast a spell?

PRE

They certainly could! Especially with that staff, if they knew how to use it. Yuri, hold on to it.

YURI

The staff? What's so dangerous about the staff?

PRE

It's a wizard's staff! (*Murgi gives the staff to Yuri, and slowly moves to the cave. Yuri puts the staff in the sack. Pre speaks to the elves.*) Now, behave yourself. Your oath.

TWOWOOs

We won't harm anyone.
We're just having some fun!

PRE

On your oath! Promise!

TWOWOOs

OK! OK!
We will, we say
Though we are really loath!
To promise on our oath!
May we sleep and never wake
If we our promise break!
(*They get back their wands. Meanwhile during this exchange, Murgi has wandered into the cave and now comes out with a mirror.*)

ARCHIE

What's that?

PRE

It's our missing mirror!! (*To the two WOOs.*) You stole it!

TWOWOOs

We didn't, we swear!
We found it in there!
In these very dark places,
We love to see our faces!

18

(They preen in front of it.)

PRE

Found it with the staff? *(The WOOs nod yes. To Archie.)* I believe
them. This was lost long ago. It's a magic mirror. But, alas, the
password was also lost, with the Great King!

ARCHIE

The Great King?

PRE

He was killed in the war. *(To Archie.)* Yes, he was the one who
started writing the tablets.

YURI

Abracadabra! *(Waves hands in front of mirror. Nothing happens!)*

MURGI

Ackle dackle doodle!

ARCHIE

No! No! Let me think. *(She thinks a moment, then looks in her
notes.)* Yes, there was a mention of a mirror. And, Penaw,
Penay…Let's see – I think it went: "Penoyourecretse"

*There is a puff of smoke and the princess appears in the mirror. She
is sitting on the floor of a cave and appears to be very weak. She
speaks in a clear, but weak, subdued voice.*

PRINCESS MIA

Oh, help me! Come quickly. I fear I'll die soon!

PRE

Princess, can you hear me?

MIA

Oh, Pre! It's you. I ran out of food wafers – my last one must've
been a year ago. I'm getting weaker and weaker.

PRE

My lady, I couldn't get here sooner. I have help now. Where're you?

MIA

A cave near the Beetle! I almost made it but they caught me and locked me in here.

MURGI

Who, my lady?

MIA

I don't know. I was knocked out and came to here. Please help me!

MURGI

We will, princess. We will! We're coming!

MIA

Please come soon. I can't last much longer.

MURGI

Just wait 'til we find who did this, princess! I'll take my axe and...

MIA

Pre, I couldn't solve the riddle. What shall I do? (*Fades away.*)

PRE

There's no time to waste. We must hurry!

A noise comes from the tunnel. They prepare for an attack, with swords, axe, wands and staffs ready. Calypso rushes in, out of breath, looking behind at the tunnel.

CALYPSO

Wow! I finally caught up to you. You were moving so quickly.

YURI

Who are you?

PRE

She's a good fairy. What is it, Calypso? You look worried.

CALYPSO

You're being followed! Scarth and Igor are tracking you. I tricked them but they won't fall for that again. You'd better leave here.

ARCHIE

Who's Scarth? Why is he following us?

CALYPSO

He's an evil member of the Dungé tribe. He's after the princess. *(The rumbling and shaking become stronger.)*

PRE

Let's go! *(They head toward the tunnel. Some rocks fall into the cave from above.)* Maybe these falling rocks will slow them down! We've got to get far away from here! *(He exits followed by Archie, Calypso, the two WOOs, Yuri and Murgi.)*

End of Scene Two.

Scene Three: *They enter a beautiful cavern with glittering crystal walls, through a crystal Archway. Paths lead to two separate exit tunnels, one with a Square crystal rim and the other with moss around the rim. There's also a cave entrance. Murgi enters followed by the WOOs, Calypso, Pre, Archie and Yuri. Murgi carries an axe, Pre his staff, Archie and Yuri swords and backpacks, and Calypso and the WOOs have wands. Yuri also has the sack with Sam's staff sticking out of it. During this scene, the WOOs tease Murgi, pulling his coat or hair, and just generally being a nuisance. He tries to ignore them.*

MURGI

Look, it's a fork in the path! Which way do we go, Pre?

TWOWOOs

Which fork will we take? What choice will we make?

WOOWON

If we take the right turn…

WOOTU

Then who knows what we'll learn?

WOOWON

If the right path we take…

WOOTU

Then t'will lead to the lake!

PRE

Quiet! Let me think a moment. It's been many many years since…

Shrieking, screaming sounds come from the passage with the square crystal rim. The Screaming Meemies come streaming in as they surround the group, except for Yuri, who pulls back toward the Archway entrance, still carrying the sack. As the Meemies encircle the cowering group, who drop to the center of the passageway floor, the two WOOs try to use their wands.

PRE

Wands don't work on them! Yuri, the sack. (*Yuri waves his sword.*)

22

YURI

Back! You'll taste my sword. Prepare to die! *(Pulls out recorder.)*

PRE

Play it! Play the recorder. *(He plays it. Meemies sink to the ground.)*

ARCHIE

(They drag them into tunnel.) Wow! That was scary. I didn't know you had such musical talent, Yuri. *(To Calypso)* What were those?

CALYPSO

Screaming Meemies. Only soothing sounds work on the Meemies. They attack when you least expect it!

ARCHIE

Pre, the princess mentioned a riddle. Is that the one about a pirate capturing a ship?

PRE

Yes! How'd you know about the riddle?

ARCHIE

I found it in the early part of the tablets. We were puzzled by it.

PRE

Oh! The great king did that.

ARCHIE

Made up a riddle? Why?

PRE

I'll explain later. Let's keep moving! *(To tunnel.)*

YURI

Going through these tunnels is nerve-wracking! Can we go up - travel aboveground?

PRE

We can, but I don't think we want to. We're safer down here.

23

ARCHIE

Why? What's wrong with going up there?

CALYPSO

It's the Flying Furies! So much has been destroyed. It's a wasteland. There's no place to hide from them. They'd see us from far away!

ARCHIE

Oh, I'm afraid to ask about the Flying Furies, but…What are they?

PRE

They're hard to describe. Hideous! Vicious! They fly like bats, silently, using radar. They have eyes like bugs and sting like bees!

ARCHIE

They sound terrible!

YURI

Calypso, you said "It's a wasteland." How'd it get to be like that?

CALYPSO

First it was the war. Each of the tribes developed such awful weapons. It was terrible! So many killed. Then the mystery! The lake. No one knows for sure. Some sort of gas.

ARCHIE

Yuri, remember those killer African lakes: Nyos, Monoon, Kivu? They found that carbon dioxide was trapped at the bottom of these deep lakes. Kivu also had methane in it.

YURI

Yes, I remember! Triggered by earthquakes or landslides. You think that happened here?

CALYPSO

A cloud came rolling across the land.

ARCHIE

See, Yuri? Just like Nyos! A crater lake!

24

CALYPSO

It killed everything! People. Animals. Everything!

PRE

Yes, everything except the Furies! I think they're some kind of mutant. They survived and you could say "they rule the skies"!

There is a thump-thump coming from the moss rimmed passageway. They draw their swords or wands and step back to the other side of the clearing. Slowly coming out of the tunnel is a giant caterpillar. He/she sees them and starts to whimper.

TENTY

Don't hurt me! Please! Don't hurt me!

MURGI

(They look at each other in amazement.) Hurt you? You have to be kidding! A big giant caterpillar like you? We're afraid you'll kill us!

TENTY

Oh, no! I wouldn't hurt a fly. I was afraid you'd make fun of me, just like everyone else!

CALYPSO

We wouldn't do that.

ARCHIE

What's your name?

TENTY

Tenty! They call me Tenty!

ARCHIE

Why do they make fun of you?

TENTY

It's because I'm always eating. I can't stop myself. That's all I want to do – eat and eat!

CALYPSO

Well, what's wrong with that?

TENTY

They call me WMD. The Worm of Mass Destruction. Then they laugh and laugh.

ARCHIE

Oh, don't worry! We won't laugh at you.

TENTY

(Shyly) I've just eaten so much, all I want to do is find a nice quiet place and build a cocoon and curl up and go to sleep. I'm so tired.

YURI

Just go in that nice quiet cave. No one will bother you there.

TENTY

Oh, thank you, thank you! *(Lumbers over to cave.)*

ARCHIE

Have a nice sleep, Tenty!

TENTY

I hope I can help you some day. *(Exits.)*

PRE

Well, that's that! Let's get on with this…(*Starts toward Square crystal-rimmed exit. A roar comes from Archway passage. The head of a Saber-toothed Tiger appears. It enters and roars again.*)

ARCHIE

What's that?

CALYPSO

It's a Saber-Toothed Tiger. Run! It's vicious! *(The group scatters. Calypso and the two WOOs exit thru the Moss tunnel. In the confusion, Calypso drops her wand in the middle of the clearing. Pre and Archie exit into the Square crystal-rimmed tunnel.)*

YURI

(Waves his sword.) Prepare to d...Aaaah! *(He runs away, following Calypso and the WOOs, thru the moss tunnel. Murgi starts to follow Archie, but just before he does, he sees Calypso's wand and yells.)*

MURGI

Calypso, you dropped your wand! *(Realizing it's too late, he grabs it and runs after Archie and Pre, barely escaping the tiger. The tiger roars again, and goes after Yuri's group thru the Moss tunnel.)*

Scarth enters thru the Archway, followed by Igor, sullen, dragging his heels. Scarth hears a distant roar from the tiger in the Moss exit.

SCARTH

I'd rather not tangle with that tiger just now. Maybe he'll do my work for me! *(Laughs.)* Let's follow this other group. Come on, you misshapen sack of scum! *(Exits)*

IGOR

(Igor starts to follow.) Yes, master! As you wish. Whatever you say. You know best! *(He goes into the tunnel briefly, but immediately darts back into the clearing.)* Master's evil! He calls me names. I'm not following him anymore! *(He looks about, sees the cave where Tenty went, and runs in there to hide. Scarth returns).*

SCARTH

Where'd you go, you wretched reptile, you villainous viper? When I find you, I'll turn you into a toadstool! *(He sees the cave, goes into it, and comes back into the clearing.)* Ugh! A giant slug! *(He looks around briefly, shrugs.)* I'll take care of you later! *(Exits.)*

IGOR

(Igor enters covered with bits of cocoon.) Aahh, it's sticky! Nasty master. I'll get back at him some day. He'll see! Umm! Which way will Igor go? *(He looks at the Moss exit, where Yuri, Calypso, the WOOs, and the tiger went; he then looks at the Square exit where Pre, Archie, Murgi and Scarth went. He moves toward the Moss exit, away from Scarth.)* Igor will take his chances with the tiger! *(Exits.)*

End of Scene Three.

Scene Four: *Yuri, Calypso and the WOOs enter a large chamber with stalactites hanging from the ceiling. Paths lead to two different exits: one is covered almost completely with moss around the rim, and the other has a high archway. The WOOs name them MOSSIE and ARCHIE. The light from MOSSIE is greater as if they were reaching the end of the long passageway they'd been following. Yuri has his sword and backpack, and the WOOs have wands, but Calypso no longer has her wand. Yuri also has the sack that Murgi gave him. They all enter out of breath from running. During this scene, the WOOs, no longer having Murgi to tease, turn their attention to Calypso. She chases them away.*

YURI
Let's rest a moment! We've outrun that beast. *(He takes off his backpack.)* I hope he didn't go back after Archie and the others. Calypso, do you know these tunnels?

CALYPSO
Not very well. I may have been here before.

YURI
Do they come back together? It looks as if another path comes in there. *(He points.)*

WOOs
Which fork do we take?
What choice do we make?

CALYPSO
I don't know! It's possible, but there are many kilometers of passages in all directions.

YURI
Should we wait here?

CALYPSO
I don't think so. We've no way of knowing where they are, or whether they're ahead of us or behind. *(The shaking and rumbling occurs again.)* Keep moving!

Yuri puts backpack on, as talking, walking, winged shrooms come in.

WOOs

Oh, what have we here!
They're poison we fear!
Our lives we hold dear!
Oh, death it is near!

YURI

What are these weird things, Calypso?

CALYPSO

They're called shrooms! Watch out! They're very dangerous! *(Yuri draws his sword and waves it.)*

YURI

Get back! You'll taste my sword! Prepare to die!

They are not impressed and move slowly closer to the group.

CALYPSO

Yuri! Don't! They're poisonous! If you slash one, its poison will splash all over us. We'll be dead in minutes. *(The WOOs whimper and cower in the middle of the clearing.)*

WOOs

If one you dare slash
Its poison will splash!

SHROOMS

(They circle the group, chanting and singing.)
Oh my, isn't this sweet? We have something to eat!
Do they taste like raw meat? Or a barrel of wheat?
Do they taste like pig's feet? Or a bog full of peat?
Well, we really don't care, we'll eat all but their hair!
Eat! Eat!
Pig's feet!
Wheat! Peat!
Sweet meat!

They close in, about to touch the group and poison them, when out of MOSSIE flies a wizard, Sam, in a flowing cape. He pulls out a wand.

SAM

Alaca balaca calaca freeze!

The shrooms freeze in place. During the following incantation, the mushrooms slowly drop to the floor all limp, as if they were melting. They end up in a puddle (pile).

To the pot we shall take
These slimy shrooms to make
A soup hot and delicious
From these creatures so vicious!
We'll slice them and dice them
Fillet them
Sauté them
Add sage and some thyme
A splash of some lime
Then to this thick broth
We'll stir to a froth
We'll have a feast fine
Of sweet shrooms divine!

WOOs

You've come to our rescue
We praise you, we thank you!
Your cape it was flowing!
Your wand it was glowing!
Oh, such a wise seer
You heard our call clear!

SAM

Here, help me drag the shrooms away. They'll make excellent soup once they're cooked. Fortunately, I happen to have a big pot in there. *(They all help drag the shrooms into the small cave. They return. Sam continues.)* I'm glad my wand worked. Haven't used it in years! *(Calypso reaches into the sack that Yuri carries, produces the staff and shows it to Sam.)*

CALYPSO
Could that be because you lost something, Sam?

SAM
My staff! Where'd you find it? *(He takes it.)*

CALYPSO
Thank the WOOS for it. They found it in a cave. How'd you lose it?

SAM
I'm too embarrassed to tell you, but thank you! Having my magic staff will make things easier. I have an important mission ahead of me. Afraid I can't stay. I'll find you later.

WOOs
We can both help too!
Can we go with you?

YURI
(Yuri responds quickly before Sam has a chance to speak.) It's alright with us. Calypso and I will manage without their help. *(Yuri and Calypso look at each other. Calypso nods.)*

SAM
(To WOOs) Well, you did find my staff. Alright. Come with me! Quickly now! *(Sam and the Woos exit the way Sam came in. Calypso is glad to get rid of the WOOs who have been a nuisance to Murgi and her ever since they were found.)*

YURI
Well, we'll just have to do without them! And their poetry! *(Yuri and Calypso smile at each other and exit via ARCHIE. The ground shakes and rumbles. More rocks fall.)*

End of Scene Four.

End of Act One.

ACT TWO

Scene One: *This setting is aboveground. There are entrances to the open ground from three places. The party enters from one side of an indentation in the cliff side. Opposite are two exits that go back below ground: one is covered with scraggly vines, and the other with abundant moss. The cliff face is in the background. The ancient city of Montoba, partially destroyed, lies before them (fourth wall) away from the cliff. The landscape in the indentation is stark and devastated before them as far as they can see. All life appears to have been destroyed. There are light clouds above them so the lighting is gray – not light and not dark. A few rocks are scattered around the otherwise barren ground. Pre enters from below ground, followed in rapid order by Archie and Murgi. He takes a deep breath from running fast. Murgi carries Calypso's wand. They still have staff, sword and axe. Shortly after they enter, Murgi sticks Calypso's wand securely in his belt.*

PRE
Whew! I think we're safe now! I haven't heard the tiger behind us. It must've chased them instead. Hope they got away!

MURGI
What a steep climb! Haven't done that for a while. Where are we?

PRE
We're at the highest point on the rim. See the long lake below?

ARCHIE
It's huge! *(Peering around.)* What are those? Sticking up all around.

PRE
The remains of towers. They were all along the inside of the rim, overlooking it. We also had many of them on the outside of the rim.

ARCHIE
How magnificent! Those towers must be half a kilometer high.

PRE
You should've seen them before the wars wrecked the city. They were twice as high. They soared over a kilometer into the sky!

ARCHIE
See the light bouncing off the solar panels – like twinkling stars!

MURGI
This city is much bigger than I imagined.

PRE
It's even bigger than what you see from here. You see only the inner city – the part that encircles the lake. The city also encircles the rim on the outside. It once stretched several kilometers in all directions.

ARCHIE
How did the people get from the outside city to the inside city?

PRE
The tunnels we've been walking in! That's what they're for. You can cross under the mountain rim through those tunnels. We also used to have gondolas that went up and over the rim. Very slow but a lovely ride. They've all been destroyed now.

MURGI
I prefer the tunnels myself.

ARCHIE
Did you see it before it was destroyed? It must've been beautiful.

MURGI
I hate to admit it, my lady, but I've never been above ground before.

ARCHIE
Never? But you seem to know all about it!

MURGI
My grandfather Gormi used to tell us stories about the city – it was our favorite bedtime tale. We'd say "tell us more, Grandpa!" We could never get enough – he told us about the high towers and the twinkling lights. It was magical. He would describe the space elevators that went high into the sky!

ARCHIE

They had space elevators too?

PRE

Yes, my lady, many. They rose several times higher than the towers.

ARCHIE

Where did they go?

PRE

To floating platforms.

MURGI

How did they stay in place in the sky?

PRE

They were connected and kept in place by a magnetic field. They were very special to us.

ARCHIE

What were they used for?

PRE

Watch towers! If the Dungé tried to attack from outside the city they could be spotted far in the distance. From that height, you could see over the rim surrounding the lake.

ARCHIE

Did they ever attack the city?

PRE

Many times! We could see many kilometers into the distance on a clear night. They always tried to attack at night. We always saw them and were ready for them.

ARCHIE

I can almost imagine the city as it was before it was destroyed. It must have been lovely.

PRE
(Nostalgically) It was full of life, teeming with activity. It was truly a vertical city. There were walkways and gardens at many levels. We had courtyards and plazas and beautiful well-kept gardens between the different towers. You could walk all around the city hundreds of feet above ground without ever touching ground level.

MURGI
And it went below ground too. My grandfather used to take us on walks around the underground city. The Midé, that was our tribe, actually mingled with the Élevé on the lower part of the city.

ARCHIE
Why didn't you go above? Wouldn't they allow you to?

MURGI
It's not that. Our people were underground people. We were more comfortable down there. We loved the nightlife in the lower city.

ARCHIE
Underground nightlife? What sort of "nightlife"? I can understand nightlife aboveground way up in the air – the plazas and walkways – but what was it like belowground?

MURGI
Well, you know we have those big caverns. We had little cafes and cabarets all around the edge of the caverns. And great beer! Do I ever miss that! Our people would gather in the center of the caverns.

ARCHIE
Just like they've done for years in the piazzas of Italy and the French plazas. What did you do for light? Wasn't it dark down there?

MURGI
Oh, no! It was sparkling. The elves gave us these magic lights that burned forever, brightly, no matter what the conditions. We were great friends with them. In some caverns, we had great stalactites hanging down and even stalagmites. The light bounced everywhere. It was magical, it was beautiful! You would have loved the old days, my lady. We had great fun. Lots of singing, and of course, drinking!

ARCHIE

I would have loved it, Murgi! Do you think any caverns still exist?

PRE

Well, the caverns may still exist, but I doubt much else does. *(There was silence. No one knew what to say next. Archie spoke again.)*

ARCHIE

Pre, what shall we do now? Where shall we go from here? I don't want to go back down there. The tiger might still be lurking below.

PRE

Well, we probably should go over there. *(He points toward the scraggly vine covered exit.)* I think it leads toward the edge of the lake. *(Archie leads the way toward the exit.)*

ARCHIE

The sooner we get moving the sooner we'll find them. *(Suddenly a giant claw sticks out and tries to grab her.)*

PRE

Watch out, Archie! Run! It's the flying crab! *(Pre pushes her away from the claw. The giant claw swings and knocks him flying into the moss-covered exit. Archie takes a step toward Pre.)*

ARCHIE

Oh, Pre! Are you hurt? *(The giant claw reaches out once again and this time grabs Archie in its claw. Murgi runs over and tries to get Archie out of the grip of the claw.)*

MURGI

My lady! I'll get you free! *(The second claw reaches out and grabs Murgi from behind. Murgi swings his axe but drops it. We see the large stinger of the crab briefly before it slowly drags the two of them back into the tunnel. As she disappears, Archie yells out.)*

ARCHIE

Oh, Yuri! Help me, help us! I've just been stung! Ohhh!

There is a short pause. Pre drags himself out of the moss covered tunnel where he was flung. He is groggy and looks around. He sees the axe and picks it up.

PRE

What happened? *(He looks around, looks quickly in the tunnel where he last saw the crab, and then up.)* The flying crab! It's taking them across the lake – must be to its lair. *(He appears to follow the flight of the flying crab as it disappears in the direction of the lake. He shakes his head.)*

PRE

There's no time to lose. I've got to find Yuri quickly. *(He summons all his strength and dashes into the scraggly vine tunnel.)*

End of Scene One.

Scene Two: *Yuri and Calypso finally exit from the passageway tunnel, and find themselves by the side of a huge lake (which stretches as far as the eye can see in the background and straight ahead of them.) There are two small boats moored next to their entrance. There is another tunnel entrance covered with brambles near them.*

YURI
Calypso, this lake seems to go on and on forever. What is it?

CALYPSO
A huge lake that replaced the mountain thousands of years ago.

YURI
What happened to the mountain?

CALYPSO
It blew up! The lake filled in the hole. Now it's surrounded by what remains of the mountain. We've been close to the lake from the start.

YURI
(Yuri mutters.) A caldera! Must've been a violent mega explosion! I wish Archie were here! It's just like Yellowstone! How big is it?

CALYPSO
Over a hundred kilometers long at least!

YURI
And half again as wide, I would say, from the looks of it.

CALYPSO
At least! But it's narrow here. And there's an island in the middle.

YURI
Gosh! What do we do now? Do we have to cross it?

CALYPSO
I'm afraid so. It'd take too long to go around. I wish Pre were here.

YURI
He's not! *(Notices boats.)* I'm glad someone left these boats nearby!

38

CALYPSO

There are boats like these all around. It's a long tradition – they're for anyone to use.

YURI

It's like our tradition. When we ran out of oil, people started using bicycles. A group got the idea of having bicycles around, for anyone to use. *(Pause. Yuri starts to help Calypso into one of the boats.)* Calypso, seeing these boats reminds me of the riddle!

CALYPSO

What riddle?

YURI

The one Archie found in the tablets. Pirates capture a ship and line up all the passengers.

CALYPSO

I thought only Pre, and the princess, knew the riddle. What is it?

YURI

There are 500 of them. The pirate chief puts his mate at the bow and tells the captain he can pick any other spot except first. The pirate chief has the numbers 2 to 7 in a tankard and says he'll pick one of the numbers at random. If it's 2 he'll throw overboard every other one and stop. The higher the number the more times through!

CALYPSO

What if the pirate chief picks three?

YURI

He throws over every 3rd, then throws over every 2nd of those left.

CALYPSO

I think I understand. What if the captain stands in thirteenth place?

YURI

He's alright if the number is 2 or 3 or even 4, but 5 will get him! *(He pauses and thinks for a moment.)* I think I've solved it!

39

CALYPSO

No one's been able to solve it!

YURI

I have. The captain has to take the correct number of paces from the bow of the ship to be safe in line. That's the clue to finding the treasure, but we need to find the start, like the bow of the ship. I think it's where this beetle is. We'd better get going!

Yuri is about to launch the boat when Pre runs in. He's out of breath and disheveled. He catches his breath. He has his staff and Murgi's axe, which he absentmindedly puts in the sack during the following.

CALYPSO

Pre! What happened? You're alone!

YURI

Where've you been? Where're Archie and Murgi?

PRE

They've been kidnapped!

CALYPSO

Kidnapped? By whom? Scarth?

PRE

No! The crab!

CALYPSO

Oh, no!

YURI

What crab?

CALYPSO

There's a huge terrible flying crab that hides in tunnels near the lake.

PRE

When we ran up the tunnel, it came out and stung Archie and Murgi.

YURI

(To himself.) Oh, Archie! *(Pause.)* What happens when they're stung? Is she hurt? Dead?

PRE

They're just unconscious! But we have to hurry before it kills them.

YURI

They're still alive! Let's go! *(Pause.)* How'd you escape?

PRE

It knocked me down and I rolled into the tunnel. When I came out, I saw the crab flying across the lake holding them in its claws.

YURI

(Comes back toward boat.) Come on! We need to cross the lake! *(Pre and Calypso don't move. Yuri's confused.)* Well? What're we waiting for? Let's not waste any more time!

CALYPSO

Yuri, it's very dangerous on the lake.

YURI

I don't care! We've got to get there before it's too late. Let's move!

They all get in one boat and start across the lake. They're in the middle of the lake when a terrifying sea monster rises up out of the water and roars. It's huge, has big eyes and nostrils, a big mouth full of sharp teeth, horns sticking up from the end of its snout, a large long tongue, and eight arms. It breathes fire! It has horny triangular projections along its back, connected with webbing. It looms overhead and then encircles the boat.

PRE

It's the Horned Draken! Get down!

The waves become larger. The Draken lets out another terrifying loud roar. It waves its eight arms to stir up the water. The boat rocks back and forth and almost overturns.

CALYPSO

We're doomed! Yuri, do something!

The Draken again rises up behind the boat. Since it wasn't able to overturn the boat, it's about to attack the boat and occupants with its tentacles. Yuri rises up, draws his sword and waves it at the beast!

YURI

Back, you beast! You'll taste my sword. Prepare to die!

Suddenly, a group of Fins enter from two directions

CALYPSO

It's the Fins! Hooray!

The Fins begin to bump and attack the Draken. The Draken roars in pain and frustration, and disappears. The Fins all talk together.

FINS

The fighting is done
The battle is won
It has made our day
To chase him away
We can think of times none
When we've had such great fun!

CALYPSO

You came just in time! Thank you! Thank you! I'm sure it would've eaten all of us in a few moments. I wish I hadn't lost my wand!

YURI

You saved our lives! Thank you!

HEAD FIN

We love to attack that oaf! He gives our lake a bad name!

CALYPSO

Is there anything we can do to repay you?

HEAD FIN
Well, when you find your wand, you can turn the Draken into a school of fish. *(The Fins laugh.)* Even with a lake as big as this, with all the poison and pollution in it, it's become hard to find enough food. *(He pauses.)* Where're you trying to get to?

PRE
We're trying to find the flying crab before it harms our friends.

YURI
Do you know where it is?

HEAD FIN
Of course! Follow us. We'll give you an escort. That ugly beast won't bother you now.

The Fins exit with the boat following. Igor runs in from the same tunnel as Yuri and the others did. He gets his breath, quickly gets in the other smaller boat and follows the others. Shortly thereafter, Scarth comes running in from the same tunnel as the one Pre entered from. He sees Igor disappearing in the last boat and shakes his fist.

SCARTH
Come back here, you cretin! If you don't, I'll find you if it's the last thing I do! I'll find the treasure and kill everyone and kill you too, you swollen bag of dung!

IGOR
Master is very angry! Igor better not go back. Master could hurt Igor if he does. Goodbye, Master!

SCARTH
You half-wit, you traitorous slime! When I catch you, I'll turn you into crab bait!

IGOR
As you wish, Master. Hee! Hee! *(Igor exits in the boat, Scarth shakes his fists at Igor and exits back into the tunnel he came from.)*

End of Scene Two.

43

Scene Three: *This setting is aboveground. There are two entrances, one through a scraggly thicket, and the other through thick moss. The landscape is stark. All vegetation has been destroyed. Light clouds above cause a gray look. A few rocks are scattered around the barren ground. Sam enters through the scraggly thicket, followed by the TWO WOOs who are out of breath. Sam is not breathing hard. They enter high on the rim above the lake. Sam faces toward the land below.*

SAM

There aren't many left after all. I see only a few scattered below.

WOOs

We don't see how
We truly fear
We can help out now
Oh, learned old seer!

SAM

You certainly can! *(To WOOWON)* Round up those people *(points down left). (To WOOTU)* Look for others there *(points down right).* Bring them together in that valley below *(points down center).*

WOOs

What is this here?
This land of fear?

SAM

We are in the outer regions of the great city. The people are scared, and don't know what to do. They need leadership. You can help by telling them what to do and where to go.

WOOs

We'll do what you say
We'll enter the fray!

SAM

Now fly! Come back quickly – and use your wands to speed them up! I'll see if I can find the Head Gryphon. *(The WOOs go in separate directions to perform their tasks. Sam whistles loudly. Soon the Head Gryphon comes in as if it flew in. It folds its wings down.)*

44

*The Gryphon is a flying creature with large wings, the head of a
condor, hind legs and hooves of a horse, and front legs and paws,
with sharp claws, like those of a lion or bird of prey. The head has a
very big sharp hooked beak. This is a friendly beast loyal to Sam.*

HEAD GRYPHON
You called, Master? What can we do to help? I'm sure that's why
you beckoned me.

SAM
You're right! Would you round up all the gryphons and any other
creatures that can carry people? We need to do an emergency
evacuation of those left. We must act quickly.

HG
I'll do as you command. May I ask where we'll take them?

SAM
To the Dark Continent!

HG
Is that not very far away?

SAM
I'm afraid so. It's several thousand kilometers.

HG
Many days journey?

SAM
You are correct. It'll take many days flying to get there with these
people. And.. *(Pauses)*

HG
And?

SAM
I'm afraid you'll not be returning.

HG

I understand. Does it have to do with the rumbling of the mountain?

SAM

You are most wise. Make haste! There's no time to lose. You leave immediately. Take everyone far from here.

HG

Where shall I assemble them?

SAM

Down below – the groups of people summoned by the WOOs are marching toward that central location.

HG

We'll soon be there. Will there be more that you want done, Master?

SAM

Yes. I have a special task for you alone. I'll meet you below to explain. And many thanks to your followers for their kind help. Mankind will owe its continued existence to them.

The Gryphon raises its wings as if to fly away and leaves on one side, while at the same time WOOWON dashes in out of breath.

WOOWON

We've completed the task
Is there more that you ask?

SAM

Yes! Take WOOTU and wait for the Head Gryphon below until it returns with the other Gryphons. You'll lead it back to Yuri and the others. I'll tell you where to meet them.

WOOWON

And why do we need
This gryphon to lead
To the group far away
And again join the fray?

SAM

There's a special job for the Gryphon to perform. I'll join you after I check on one last location. *(Sam pauses.)* Oh, one last thing! Take this with you. Give it to Pre.

He reaches into his pocket and takes out a magic ball. He gives it to WOOWON.

WOOWON

And what is this ball?
Perhaps for a wall?

SAM

You continue to amaze me! *(He shakes his head.)* I don't understand why Yuri and Calypso let you go so easily. You've been such a great help! *(WOOWON smiles and leaves on one side while Sam leaves on the other.)*

End of Scene Three.

Scene Four: *Pre, Yuri and Calypso have crossed the lake, which is now behind them. They enter with the boat and beach it. All the rest of the stage is land. A bridge crosses from land to edge of water and under it is a cave-like tunnel through which a river comes into the lake. A troll lives under the bridge. A passageway leads to a cave in which the crab has taken its captives. There is also a worn path from the beach entry point to another passageway overgrown with vines.*

PRE, CALYPSO and YURI
Goodbye! Thank you again! *(They wave offstage to Fins.)*

YURI
What's in here? *(He goes in to the tunnel under the bridge.)*

PRE
Let's check out the caves. Calypso, you take that one! *(Points to tunnel where main path leads.)* I'll take this one! *(Points to cave. They exit. Yuri returns, dragging a troll by the hand.)*

ROLLY
Etlay emay elphay onyay!

YURI
What? I can't understand you!

ROLLY
Eymay amenay siay ollyray! Oh, sorry, my name is Rolly. Let me help you! I'm a friend. *(Calypso returns from the tunnel talking.)*

CALYPSO
It's the main passageway. It keeps going. *(Sees Rolly.)* Who are you?

ROLLY
I'm Rolly. I want to help you.

YURI
And what are you? What kind of creature are you?

ROLLY
Oh, I'm a troll. I thought you knew that. I'm a friend. Can I help?

48

YURI

We're looking for a giant crab. It flys and…*(Rolly holds up his hands to stop Yuri, and points to the cave tunnel where Pre went.)*

ROLLY

Say no more! That way! It lives in a cave there. I hate that beast!

YURI

Lead the way. We'll follow.

ROLLY

I'll show you where it is, but I won't go in. It's very dangerous!

YURI

We must go in! I just hope it's not too late. *(He starts toward the tunnel to the cave just as Pre comes backing out, holding his nose.)*

PRE

I found its lair. Smells of crab! Ugh!

YURI

(To Rolly) You said you could help. How?

ROLLY

If I get it out in the open, will that help?

PRE

Yes, I think so – how will you do that?

ROLLY

Wait here! *(He dashes in to his cave under the bridge, comes out with a wafer – pale green – and holds it in his hands.)* Otay ottenray eatmay! *(It turns into a chunk of old rotten meat.)* I'll be back in a minute! Be ready! *(He puts the meat on a long stick and exits into the tunnel where the crab lurks.)*

CALYPSO

What's he doing?

YURI

Yes, what on earth was that?

PRE

The crab loves rotten meat! The troll turned a wafer into the meat. We'd better keep an eye on him. With those kinds of tricks, no telling what he'll do next.

Rolly returns backing out of the tunnel entrance holding the meat in front of him. The others back away to the sides of the clearing as Rolly leads the giant flying crab into the center of the clearing. It has long legs, giant claws, giant wings and a large unicorn horn in the middle of its head, which can sting and make anyone unconscious. Yuri draws his sword to get ready to fight the crab.

YURI

Back, back! My sword'll turn you to crab bisque. Prepare to die!

Calypso reaches for her wand and realizes it's gone. Pre readies his staff. Yuri dashes around the crab and into the tunnel. The crab realizes it's been tricked. As it turns, Calypso sees an opportunity.

CALYPSO

Quick, Pre, your staff!

Pre goes behind it and touches the back of the crab's neck, where its weak spot is, with his staff. The crab goes into death spasms, rolls over, and dies with its feet in the air.

PRE

That takes care of it. Let's drag it into the sea, where it belongs!

They drag the carcass to the edge of the sea and roll it in (offstage).

CALYPSO

That should feed the Fins for some time!

YURI

(Yuri comes rushing out, holding Archie in his arms.) Murgi's lying in there! Pre, is Archie dead? *(Pre feels her head.)*

PRE

No, she's still alive, but barely. No time to lose! Where's your sack? *(Yuri shows him where he dropped it to fight the crab. Pre reaches in and pulls out some wafers, and gives Yuri a pink one. Rolly watches this with great interest!)* Here, give her this. Come on, Calypso! *(They run into the tunnel.)*

YURI

(Yuri holds Archie in his arms and puts the pink wafer into her mouth to revive her.) Oh, Archie! I'm sorry. I never should have left you. Please don't die!

ARCHIE

(She revives slowly.) Yuri! Where am I? What happened? Oh, I remember. That awful crab. Where is it?

YURI

Don't worry, Arch! It's dead. Archie, I thought you were a goner.

ARCHIE

So did I! *(She hugs him. Pre comes out holding Murgi, and reaches into the sack for another pink wafer. Calypso comes out holding her wand.)*

CALYPSO

I found my wand!

PRE

Never mind now about the wand. Here, give this to Murgi! *(He gives the wafer to Calypso. She puts it in Murgi's mouth.)* He'll be alright in a minute. Wow, that was close!

YURI

What happened, Archie?

ARCHIE

A huge claw grabbed me and dragged me into a tunnel. The last thing I remember was being stung. I thought for sure that was it.

YURI
Thank heavens we got to you in time. Where were you anyway?

ARCHIE
Oh, Yuri! What a sight! When we came aboveground, I could see the remains of the old city. There are still sections towering high into the air, and some solar energy panels. Even now the city twinkles and soars high in the air. They really did it! It's true! This must have been a magnificent city! *(Tears come to her eyes.)*

PRE
(Murgi begins to wake up.) Let's get away from the lake and the open ground. I feel safer down in the tunnel. *(He helps Murgi to his feet. He is groggy and unsteady.)*

MURGI
Uhhh! Where? Where are we? What happened?

CALYPSO
On the other side of the lake. Are you all right, Murgi? I missed you.

MURGI
I'm alright I guess. I lost my axe! *(He realizes he has lost his axe and her wand in his belt.)* And your wand! I was keeping it for you, after you dropped it.

CALYPSO
(She shows him her wand.) Thank you for looking after it. I found it in there. *(She points. She can't resist teasing him.)* Lost your axe, huh? Pretty careless! *(Meanwhile she reaches into the sack and pulls out his axe.)* You can thank Pre for this.

MURGI
My axe! I don't remember much. What happened?

CALYPSO
We'll tell you on the way! The important thing is that you're alright!

PRE
Let's go! *(He starts toward the tunnel.)*

ROLLY

Can I go with you?

YURI

Of course! After helping save Archie and Murgi, you're a true
friend. *(Pre gives Yuri a look of caution then shrugs.)*

PRE

Well, alright. Let's get away from here! *(They exit into the tunnel.
Pre leads, followed by Archie, Yuri, Murgi and Calypso. Archie still
has her backpack which was on her back during the attack by the
crab, and Yuri has his backpack on his back and the sack in his
hand. Rolly eyes the sack covetously. Calypso now has her wand and
Murgi now has his axe, and Pre his staff. Rolly is last. He rubs his
hands together, smiling as he follows.)*

ROLLY

I'm a true friend, he says!

*As they exit the rumbling and shaking is more violent than ever
before. Shortly after they exit, Igor comes in with the other boat and
beaches it next to their boat. He gets out, looks around at all the
other caves and tunnels.*

IGOR

Igor doesn't like Master anymore. Igor will call him Scarth, bad
Scarth! *(He straightens up with pride.)* Igor will be brave. Scarth
wants to steal the princess and the treasure, and kill the others. Igor
won't let him. He'll get there first and warn them. *(He follows them.)*

End of Scene Four.

Scene Five*: There are several rocks near the walls of this clearing. There are two caves partially covered with vines. They had entered through a moss-covered entryway. A well-travelled path led to another passage almost completely covered with vines. The group (Pre, Archie, Yuri, Murgi, Calypso and Rolly) enter slowly.*

ARCHIE
I'm tired! Can we rest for a moment?

PRE
Alright, but not for long! We're getting close to where I think the princess is trapped!

Rolly continues to have his eye on the sack that Yuri carries. He slides in to the nearby tunnel and just before he exits, he pops a pale green wafer into his mouth. He is observed only by Pre!

PRE
Yuri! Murgi! I think we may have trouble here. I don't like the looks of this. Rolly can't keep his eyes off the sack. He just disappeared into that cave.

Before he can continue, there is a rumble and shaking. A giant troll slowly lumbers out of the cave where Rolly went. It is holding a giant club and making low rumbling roaring noises. They all move to the sides of the clearing with swords, staffs and wands at hand.

MURGI
Look out! It's a giant troll.

ARCHIE
It must be Rolly! He disappeared into that tunnel.

PRE
It is! I saw him take that green wafer before he left.

The troll moves to the center of the clearing. Yuri is near the tunnel exit with the sack in his hand. The troll advances slowly toward Yuri with club in hand.

YURI

Back, you beast! *(Grabs his sword.)*

PRE

Run, Yuri! He wants the sack!

YURI

He'll taste my sword first. Prepare to die! *(Raises his sword to fight.)*

ARCHIE

Don't be foolish, Yuri! It's too big! Get back!

A giant cabbage skunk enters from the entrance tunnel. The cabbage skunk is an ancient ancestor of both the skunk cabbage and the common skunk. It is very large, has black and white stripes all over its body and legs, except for its head, which is bright yellow, like the new growth of the skunk cabbage. It has an overwhelming stench.

YURI

What a stink! *(Holds his nose.)* What is it?

PRE

It's a cabbage skunk. Keep out of the way.

The troll hears the skunk enter, turns away from Yuri and faces the skunk. The skunk circles up and the troll follows its movements. The cabbage skunk stinks so strongly that the troll cannot stand the smell and backs up slowly away from it, where, unseen by the troll, a large walking ivy enters. The ivy comes up behind the troll, wraps its long tendrils around the troll and holds it.

YURI

You guys are doing fine! *(Puts his sword away.)*

The cabbage skunk advances on the troll and the troll passes out from the strong stench. The ivy drags the troll away into the cave it came from. The cabbage skunk shrugs and walks back into the tunnel it came from. The astonished group moves to the center of the clearing.

ARCHIE

You called it a cabbage skunk. What's that!? *(Points to tunnel where cabbage skunk exited.)* It looks like a cross between a skunk cabbage and a skunk, but how can that be?

PRE

Evolution's a strange thing! It's probably an ancient ancestor of your two different species. This one's a plant eating mammal and lives close to the edge of our lake.

ARCHIE

And the other one? *(Points to where the ivy dragged the troll.)*

PRE

Oh, that! That one's carnivorous, a meat eating plant. I've only seen one other. They're rare. We consider them an endangered species.

YURI

Well, what is it then? The plant thing I mean. *(Points at the exit.)*

CALYPSO

It's an ivy plant.

PRE

It's evolved too. When its habitat aboveground was destroyed, it evolved into a walking carnivorous plant that lives belowground.

MURGI

Enough about all this evolution stuff! Let's get going! Our princess is in peril! We must save her. *(He leads into the tunnel and the others follow.)*

A short while later, Igor comes into the clearing, looks around and listens. He hears the departing group in the distance, but hears an ominous sound – footsteps that have been behind him. He quickly slides into a cave and waits. Slowly, into the clearing, a tired and exhausted Scarth enters, shuffling slowly, but trying his best to keep up with the footsteps he's heard. He listens, goes into the tunnel where the group has gone. Igor comes quietly out of hiding.

IGOR
I need to slow him down. It worked once. Maybe it will again. Then I'll follow him! That's a much better plan.

Igor uses his staff to make noises in the other cave to draw Scarth back into the clearing and slow him up. Igor goes back into his cave. The plan works because soon Scarth comes back and goes into the cave where noises can still be heard. In a moment he comes back out, shaking his head angrily.

SCARTH
That traitorous tricky cretin must have something to do with this! If I ever catch that slimy rotten walking bag of dung, I'll turn him into a tiny beetle and squash him with my foot! *(He returns to the tunnel again following the group. Igor then comes back out.)*

IGOR
It worked! Now all I have to do is follow quietly and wait for my chance! *(He follows.)*

End of Scene Five.

End of Act Two.

ACT THREE

Scene One: *They enter another underground clearing after leaving the shores of the lake. They finally reach the cave where the princess is held captive behind a wall of thick ivy branches with thorns. In front of the cave entrance is a formidable river of red molten lava. Another tunnel enters close to the river of lava and a third leads down from the ground level above. Murgi is the first to come running in from there to the clearing and stops when he sees the lava river ahead.*

MURGI
Hello? Anyone here? *(He listens for a sound.)*

PRINCESS MIA
(After a pause, a weak voice answers.) Is someone out there? Hello?

MURGI
(Realizing the voice is coming from behind the wall of thorns and brambles and ivy.) Princess, is that you? Behind the thorns?

MIA
Murgi! It's you! I've been trapped here a long time. Are you alone?

MURGI
No, Pre and the others are just behind me. Are you alright?

MIA
I'm very weak, but I'm alright! Be careful! They'll be back soon!

MURGI
Who, my princess?

MIA
The heads!

MURGI
Heads, my lady? *(Pre, Yuri, Archie and Calypso enter.)* Here's Pre!

PRE
Is our princess here?

58

MURGI

Yes, she's in there, behind the thorns! *(Points.)* She's very weak!

PRE

(Calls to her.) Princess?

MIA

Oh, Pre! *(Her voice gets a little stronger.)* I'm so glad you made it.
Please get me out of here. I can't last much longer. I haven't eaten in
so long…*(Her voice trails off.)*

PRE

Yuri, quick! An orange wafer! *(Yuri reaches in and pulls out an
orange wafer.)* Can you throw it straight? Through the thorns?

YURI

Just watch! *(He throws it across the lava river through the thorns.)*

MIA

I've got it! I've got it! Thank heavens! *(Pauses while she devours it.)*
Pre, can you get me out of here?

PRE

We'll need help getting over the river, but we'll figure it out.

CALYPSO

Where is that wizard when you need him?

MURGI

What are we going to do?

PRE

(Puts his hand to brow.) Let me think!

MIA

Pre, be careful! It'll be back any moment!

PRE

It? What do you mean?

MIA

The beast! It never leaves for very long. It's been guarding this cave for a very long time. It's due back any minute.

YURI

I'll take care of it, whatever it is! *(He draws his sword.)*

ARCHIE

Yuri! Not again. Put your sword away.

MIA

Oh, be careful! It's very dangerous. I think I hear it coming back!

There's a rumbling sound as the two headed gorgon lumbers in from the cave at the lower part of the clearing. It is a two-headed creature with snakes for hair and eyes that can turn beholders to stone. Each head roars in sequence, first head one, then the second, then both.

PRE

(He turns away.) Don't look at its eyes! Turn away! *(They all turn.)*

ARCHIE

What is it?

PRE

A two-headed gorgon!

YURI

What's that?

PRE

It'll turn you to stone if you look in its eyes! Follow me! We have to get away from here!

He exits through the tunnel to open ground. Archie and Yuri follow.

MURGI

We'll be back soon, Princess, to get you out! *(He moves to the exit and hesitates.)*

MIA

Take care of yourself first, Murgi!

CALYPSO

We will, we will! Go, Murgi!

She pushes him into the tunnel and follows. The gorgon lumbers after them slowly.

End of Scene One.

Scene Two: *This setting is aboveground. There are entrances to the open ground from a few passages. The landscape is again devastated. There are light clouds in the distance and the lighting is gray. There are a few rocks scattered around. Pre enters thru an opening covered with scraggly thickets. He's followed in rapid order by Archie, Yuri, Murgi, and Calypso. They all take a deep breath from running so fast.*

PRE
Whew! That was close! Everyone here?

YURI
I think so! *(Looks around.)* Yes! What'll we do now?

PRE
Yuri, do you still have that mirror in your sack?

YURI
Yes, here it is! *(Yuri pulls it out and shows him.)*

PRE
Great! Be ready. We may need it. I have an idea. *(Yuri has it ready.)*

ARCHIE
If the gorgon looks in the mirror, will it turn itself to stone?

CALYPSO
No, I'm afraid not! It's immune. A few people are immune to the stare as well, such as the princess.

MURGI
So then, what can we do with the mirror?

PRE
Protect us from its stare. Deflect it. My idea is to get close in and try to cut off a head or two with one of the swords. I'm not sure it'll work, but it's worth a try!

MURGI
We have to do something!

Just then, the gorgon comes up out of the tunnel. They all turn away and head in the opposite direction. However, at that moment, from all directions, the Flying Furies fly in and land on the ground, surrounding them. The Furies are ferocious winged creatures resembling a cross between a bat, bee and bug.

CALYPSO
Oh, no! The Flying Furies! I was afraid of this!

ARCHIE
We're trapped! We're done for!

They all turn back toward the gorgon, which looks at them, and they all make the mistake of looking at it. Calypso yells but it's too late.

CALYPSO
Don't look!

They all turn to stone in the middle of the open ground. The Furies realize the group is now stone, go around them, and, in their fury, attack the gorgon's eyes until it can no longer see. The gorgon tries to escape in the opposite direction from where it came in, and the Furies go after it. A giant moth comes up out of a tunnel, and with its wings spread, goes after the Furies. The Furies scatter in fear of this giant creature, and the gorgon also slinks off, glad to be alive. The giant moth goes over to Archie, touches her and dusts her with magic moth dust. He does the same with all the stone statues. Each of them begins to return to life. The first one touched was Archie.

ARCHIE
Oh, what happened?

GIANT MOTH
You were turned to stone.

ARCHIE
Your voice. You sound very much like someone we met before.

TENTY
It's not surprising.

ARCHIE

Tenty! You sound like Tenty.

TENTY

I am Tenty, my lady.

ARCHIE

Oh, Tenty! You saved us. *(The others gradually wake up.)*

TENTY

You helped me when it was important. I'm glad to return the favor.

MURGI

What happened? Who's this?

ARCHIE

We were turned to stone. It's Tenty! He saved us.

YURI

How?

TENTY

Just a little magic moth dust! You see, amongst our kind, you could say I'm the prince of moths. *(Pause as he looks around.)* What're you doing up here anyway?

MURGI

We were being chased, but I don't remember what happened.

TENTY

It's not safe! I was lucky there were only a few Furies and I chased them away. You should get below.

YURI

Good idea! *(He moves to the tunnel.)* What happened to the gorgon?

TENTY

The Furies put out its eyes. It crawled away. It won't harm anyone anymore.

ARCHIE

Aren't you coming with us?

TENTY

No! *(Spreads its wings to fly away.)* I have some business to attend to. I have to find a mate pretty soon and let nature takes its course. Goodbye! *(It moves away from both the furies and the tunnel.)*

CALYPSO, MURGI, PRE

Goodbye, Tenty! And thank you! *(They head to the tunnel exit.)*

YURI

And good luck! *(He follows.)*

ARCHIE

Take care, Tenty! *(Tenty and the others exit. Archie is the last to exit.)*

End of Scene Two.

Scene Three: *This is the same setting as in ACT Three, Scene One. The princess is still in the cave behind the wall of thorns. They enter.*

PRE

Princess, are you alright?

MIA

Yes, Pre, I'm feeling better. What happened? I was afraid the gorgon would get you!

PRE

It did! We got trapped between it and the Furies, but we were lucky.

MIA

What do you mean? How did you escape?

PRE

The Furies got the gorgon's eyes, and an old friend came to our rescue. We're all alright!

MIA

I'm glad of that. I feel so helpless here.

MURGI

What're we going to do now? We've got to get the princess out.

PRE

I'm thinking.

TWO WOOs walk in, leading the Gryphon, carrying the magic ball.

TWOWOOS

Have no fear!
WOOs are here!
Through the dangers, never lose!
To the rescue come the WOOs!

CALYPSO

Well, look what we have here! You weren't so brave when the shrooms attacked us!

YURI

What's that? *(Points to Gryphon.)*

WOOWON

The Gryphon's on loan
It's not one we own
Yet it's free to roam
But it has no home!

YURI

Your rhymes are getting pretty pathetic!

TWOWOOS

We've become so meek
'Cause we're getting weak
We have reached our peak
Now it's food we seek!

YURI

I'll give you a food wafer! *(He reaches into his sack and gives each of them an orange food wafer.)* What's that? In your hand?

WOOTU

We heard your loud call
Sam sent you the ball
To knock down the wall
To free one and all!

PRE

So that's what Sam meant. He must have known about the lava river and the wall of thorns! Well, let's give it a try! *(Pre gets on the back of the Gryphon, takes the magic ball in one hand and they jump over the river of lava. He rolls the ball against the wall and it parts. He goes in and comes out a moment later carrying Princess Mia.)*

MIA

Pre, you're my savior! *(She kisses him. There's a puff of smoke. Pre disappears. The prince stands in his place.)*

PRINCE PETER
My darling Mia! I'm free at last from Scarth's spell! *(Peter hugs her, lifts her onto the back of the Gryphon. They jump over the lava.)*

MIA
Peter? Prince Peter, is it really you?

PETER
Yes, my princess, you're safe now!

MIA
Oh, Peter! What happened to you? I've missed you so much.

PETER
Scarth turned me into a leprechaun. He wanted you for himself.

MIA
Never! I'd die first before I'd allow him to kiss me. It's you I've always wanted, Peter!

PETER
Scarth thought, if he had you, he could rule the whole world.

MURGI
And don't forget the treasure. He wanted the treasure too.

PETER
Well, he can't have either. We'll see to that!

MIA
Let's go find the Beetle! *(The WOOs lead the Gryphon away.)*

PETER
Lead the way! *(Scarth enters from the tunnel they all entered from, with staff in hand. The WOOs have managed to escape before Scarth enters. The WOOs have disappeared, with the Gryphon in tow.)*

SCARTH
Not so fast! I have you where I want you! I see you're finally free of my spell. It won't make any difference. *(Scarth raises his staff.)*

IGOR

(Igor comes running in from the tunnel behind Scarth and grabs Scarth's staff.) Not so fast yourself, Master Scarth! I'll be the Master now! *(Igor starts to put a spell on Scarth.)*

PETER

Hold it, Igor! Let's give him a fair chance. Yuri, give him your sword. What will it be, Scarth? Fight or run? *(Yuri looks at Peter and reluctantly hands his sword to Scarth.)*

SCARTH

(He takes the sword before he says anything.) Hmmm, one of my followers is blind, thanks to the Furies! Now one of them has become a traitor. *(He looks at Igor who looks boldly back at him.)*

PETER

You're the traitor! Stand and fight!

SCARTH

I still have one ally left! Abersay, Igertay! *(The Saber-Toothed Tiger comes from aboveground and roars. Archie draws her sword.)*

ARCHIE

(To Peter.) You take care of him, I'll take care of this beast! It's time to show women can fight as well as men!

There is a furious fight between all four while the others get out of the way. The fighting goes back and forth. Yuri yells to Archie.

YURI

Do you need some help? *(Archie chases the tiger back into the tunnel and gives Yuri a dirty look.)*

The battle between Scarth and Peter continues longer, but eventually Peter wounds Scarth severely, so he backs up to the tunnel from above ground. The blind gorgon, which can still smell, reaches in, grabs Scarth and drags him away, as he screams. Igor sees the end of Scarth, rubs his hands together in satisfaction, and unnoticed by anyone, slips into the entrance tunnel from which he came.

ARCHIE

(She sheathes her sword. To Peter.) What took you so long? *(He smiles, sheathes his.)*

MURGI

Well, now can we go to the Beetle? If you warriors are through with your competition!? *(Archie gives Murgi a playful arm hug. Sam walks into the clearing.)*

CALYPSO

Look who's here? What took you so long? *(Sam smiles.)*

PETER

Leave it to a wizard to show up after all the action is over!

SAM

I see you're free and feisty as ever! All of you! *(Sam looks at Peter and Mia, as well as Calypso and Murgi.)* If you must know, we've been saving a few hundred people and creatures. You're the last ones left around here. I wish we had more time to banter, but we must leave quickly. *(Sam looks around.)* Where are the WOOs?

MURGI

They left with the Gryphon before the battle. What are we waiting for? *(Sam frowns.)*

SAM

Hmmm! I saw the Gryphon up there but no WOOs. Oh well, they'll turn up! Let's go find that Beetle! *(The group follows Mia back out of the tunnel they all originally came through. The ground rumbles and shakes violently, and several rocks fall.)*

End of Scene Three.

Scene Four: *The treasure site. The Beetle is center with sky in the background. Cliffs surround the clearing. At one end brambles and vines conceal a cave. The light is now brighter than ever before. Mia, Peter, Archie, Calypso, Murgi, and Yuri enter from the other end.*

MIA
Looks as if no one found this site while I was gone! Just as I left it!

YURI
What happened to those mischievous WOOs?

MIA
They ran ahead but I don't think they know how to get here!

PETER
Where can they be? I hope they're not lost!

ARCHIE
They're off somewhere getting into trouble. They'll be back.

MURGI
My lady? Where's the treasure?

MIA
I don't know! I tried to solve the riddle on my way. It tells where the treasure is. All I know is that it's not too far from the beetle.

YURI
That's it! The beetle's the ship in the riddle! I'll find the treasure! *(He stands at the front of the beetle, and paces toward the cave.)*

PETER
What's he doing? Where's he going? *(They watch him go in.)*

CALYPSO
I think he solved the riddle. He figured out the number of paces the captain takes. That's where the treasure must be hidden.

ARCHIE
That's what it's all about! Yuri did it! *(Yuri returns with a sack.)*

71

YURI

It's in the back of that cave. Sacks and sacks! What'll we do with it?

MIA

Thank heavens! Put it in the beetle, please! Murgi, will you help?

MURGI

Of course, my lady. *(Yuri, Peter, Calypso and Murgi enter the cave.)*

ARCHIE

Princess, what's in the treasure? It doesn't seem to be gold or silver.

MIA

They're no value here. It's sacks and sacks of wafers we invented!

ARCHIE

Wafers? You mean like these? *(She reaches into the sack Yuri left when he went to help, and she pulls out a few different wafers.)*

MIA

Yes, we've lots of food wafers. *(Holds up orange one).* You know about those. Yuri threw one through the thorns. Thanks heavens he did! And we've lots of fuel wafers. *(She holds up a tan one.)*

ARCHIE

Fuel wafers?

MIA

The Beetle uses them as we use food wafers. Each lasts a year, more if the Beetle shuts down. It's like hibernation. *(Holds a white wafer.)*

ARCHIE

What's that white one for?

MIA

This is our greatest invention! You'd call it an anti-aging wafer.

ARCHIE

Anti-aging?

MIA

Yes, it slows down aging dramatically! For these long space voyages, we needed them. We live a very long time anyway but this is something special! Our bodies go into a kind of long hibernation. We wake up periodically when our bodies run out of fuel.

ARCHIE

Did you say "we"?

MIA

Yes, Peter's going with me! *(They put the wafers back except for one that Archie holds up: a yellow wafer. The others have been loading sacks and sacks into the Beetle and finally stop and come over.)*

ARCHIE

What's this yellow one for?

MIA

Oh, that one's very special! *(Before she answers, Peter interrupts. Archie absentmindedly puts it in Yuri's backpack, next to the sack.)*

PETER

Well, that's it! We got all of them! Are you ready? Where's Sam?

SAM

(Just then Sam walks in with the Gryphon.) You called? *(At this point the ground shakes more violently than ever.)* Time to leave here! Quickly! Calypso! Murgi! You're going with me on the Gryphon! Far from here!

MIA

Yes, the sooner we get away from this place the better. We don't have much time from the sounds of it! The explosion's coming! Calypso! Murgi! Sam! When you find the WOOs will you take them away from here as fast as you can?

MURGI and CALYPSO

Yes, my lady!

73

SAM

Don't worry about the WOOs! They'll look after themselves!

MIA

Goodbye! *(She hugs them.)* And take care of yourselves!

PETER

(To Yuri and Archie.) Those two wafers you saved? Eat them.
*(Everyone hugs everyone else. Mia and Peter enter the Beetle,
Calypso and Murgi follow Sam off muttering to themselves.)*

MURGI

Those pesky WOOs!

CALYPSO

Where can they be? *(They exit off.)*

SAM (Off)

Acalaphon! Gryphonala! Away! *(We hear the Gryphon taking off.)*

ARCHIE

Yuri, ever think what might have happened if we hadn't come?

YURI

You mean what did! Don't forget that! Good thing I ate that wafer!

ARCHIE

The course of history changed? Scarth would be on the Beetle now?

YURI

Who can say? Anyway, let's get out of here before this thing blows!

*They each pop a wafer into their mouth. There is a roar as the Beetle
takes off and a puff of smoke as Yuri and Archie disappear. All goes
dark. There is silence followed by the roar of violent explosions as
the lake and mountain explode in deafening cataclysmic sounds.*

End of Scene Four.

End of Act Three.

EPILOGUE: *Archie sitting. Yuri comes in. Backpacks on the floor.*

YURI

Hi, Arch! *(She looks at him expectantly.)* No, I still don't know!

ARCHIE

We've been back two weeks. You still can't fix the time it'll arrive?

YURI

Archie, I can fix it but the whole thing doesn't make sense!

ARCHIE

What do you mean?

YURI

When we came back here the clock hadn't changed, even though we were gone for months. Everything's the same as when we left!

ARCHIE

So? Maybe it was all a dream? Is that what you think?

YURI

For both of us? No. You've heard of parallel universes? Maybe we just dropped into a parallel timeframe, but remembered everything!

ARCHIE

Well, alright! Maybe! So, what's your problem then?

YURI

Archie, time didn't stop for the object. I know when it should arrive!

ARCHIE

When?

YURI

February 26th! But how could time keep moving for it and not us?

ARCHIE

Well, you said it! A different time space! *(He frowns.)* What else?

YURI

Archie, I'm not sure you're going to believe me!

ARCHIE

Try me!

YURI

It looks like the Beetle!

ARCHIE

(She jumps up.) Is the telescope set up? Can I look at it?

YURI

Go ahead! Tell me what you think! *(She runs off. He reaches into his backpack, feels the yellow wafer, and holds it up. Archie returns.)*

ARCHIE

Sure looks like it! Is it possible they're still on it? Still alive?

YURI

We'll find out soon enough. Someone or something is making it change direction as it gets closer. Archie?

ARCHIE

Yes?

YURI

What's this? A yellow wafer? I've never seen this before.

ARCHIE

Yes! It's special. Mia was about to tell me. I wonder what it's for?

YURI

Well, there's one way to find out! *(He holds it near his mouth.)*

ARCHIE

(She leaps to him.) Yuri! No! *(He puts it down.)*

YURI

Just kidding, Arch! *(He pauses and thinks for a moment.)* Archie?

ARCHIE

Yes?

YURI

What do you suppose happened to those WOOs?

ARCHIE

I've wondered about that! They were very clever, you know!
Maybe...?

End of Epilogue and End of Play.

APPENDIX A

Costume Design / Costumes (Suggested or minimal) – Re-use heads and wings

ARCHIE and YURI (Futuristic - Silver Lightweight Lame or Gortex outfits - formfitting)
PRE (Leprechaun) – Green Outfit with a little dusty brown
MURGI (Gnome) – Dark, Underground Miner Look
SCARTH (An evil hooded figure) – Black Hooded
IGOR (Goblin) – Ugly ragtag look
CALYPSO (Fairy) – Wings and ballerina skirt
TWO WOOs (Elves) – Dark matching outfits, tapered legs and pointed shoes
PRINCESS MIA – Lovely, elegant outfit but dirty and worn
SCREAMING MEEMIES (4 or more) – ratty, tattered skirts with big dark eyes
TENTY (Caterpillar) (4 or more in 1) – Head of sweet face and antlers plus sheet
SABER-TOOTHED TIGER (2 in 1) – Head with teeth and ears plus sheet
SHROOMS (4 or more) – Caps with flared outfits, mushroom shaped – wings optional
SAM (Wizard) – Flowing cape and pointed wizard hat
FLYING UNICORN CRAB (3 in 1) – As described, wings, big claws and stinger in head
HORNED DRAKEN (Several in 1) – Head from tiger with horns and just about anything
FINS (4 or more) – Dolphin Fish Faces
GRYPHON (2 in 1) – As described, bird head, wings, claws on feet
ROLLY (Troll) – Droll Troll, Underground Look
GIANT TROLL – Big lumbering ugly drab beast
GIANT CABBAGE SKUNK – Black and white striped body with yellow head
WALKING IVY – Vines dangling all around and from hands
TWO-HEADED GORGON (2 in 1) – Big penetrating eyes and tangled hair like snakes
FLYING FURIES (4 or more) – As described. wings with big eyes, dark look, ugly

GIANT MOTH (3 in 1) – Dusky look with fluffy wings and body – likeable moth
PRINCE PETER – Old fashioned prince look
FLYING BEETLE (2) – Storyboard Drawing with feet sticking out at bottom that move

Note: The idea is to use minimal, imaginative and suggested simple costumes – all characters are identified in dialogue so have fun with these costumes, and don't make a big costume production shop!! In the initial staging and rehearsals, the cast consisted of students from both middle school and high school, and was done in conjunction with the art department. Most students created their own costumes.

APPENDIX B

Set Design, Pieces and Effects (Suggested ideas used in staging)

Two Chairs, Table and Lamp
Entrances to caves and tunnels – inserts into black box (black curtain) entrances made of 2x2s covered with "cave stone" paper – covered and uncovered as needed in scenes
Markings and Engravings in Back Wall (Storyboard)
Worn pathways in underground clearings – paper track with worn steps – moveable
Sea in background (Storyboard) and Floor Sides
Waves – fixed foldable plywood across stage with hidden crew holding rocking waves
Boats – cardboard held by cast upstage and carried with one hand
River of Lava – painted paper
Wall of Thorns – netting augmented
Flying Beetle (Storyboard) with two pairs of cast feet below on sides – think Mandelbrot Set as beetle shape

Note: To make various caverns and clearings look slightly different use imaginative ideas such as in novel with rocks, moss, crystal or stalactites/stalagmites.

APPENDIX C

Prop Design / Prop List

Thin slate like sheets (tablets)- laptop
Magnifying Glass
Journal and Pen (Archie)
Journal and Pen (Yuri)
Backpacks (Archie and Yuri)
Photographs (Yuri)
Letter
Wafers (Necco)
>   Gray (Time)
>   Orange (Food)
>   Pink (Anti-venom)
>   Pale Green (Transmogrification)
>   Tan (Fuel)
>   White (Aging)
>   Yellow
Staff - Leprechaun
Axe – Gnome- made of paper mache
Sack (burlap)
Two swords (rapiers)- made of wood and painted
Recorder
Staff- Scarth
Staff - Igor
Wands- Calypso, two WOOs
Staff – Sam
Mirror
Rocks- Paper Mache (thrown over flats by crew – they had fun doing this!)
Bits of Cocoon cotton
Two small boats - cardboard
Waves (see previous appendix)
Small club – Rolly (paper mache)
Piece of (Fake) Raw Meat
Large Club – Troll
Magic Ball

APPENDIX D

Special Effects, Sound Effects and Music

Noise and smoke when Yuri disappears- used smoke machine
Similar situation when Princess vision is seen in mirror
Rumbling and Shaking of mountain – small earthquakes
Sounds of rocks falling when rocks fall
Similar situation to first two when Pre turns into Prince
Roar of explosion of super volcano

(Optional or can be done by cast)

Offstage sounds by wands of Calypso and Igor
Music when Scarth and Igor approach
Screaming Meemies sounds
Tenty music
Roar of saber-toothed tiger
Noises of talking shrooms
Dragon Roar
Talking Fins
Approach of Crab
Approach of Giant Troll
Gorgon sounds
Flying Furies sounds
Gryphon approach, jumping and flying away

MONTOBA – SCENES and CHARACTERS

ACT->		I	I	I	I	II	II	II	II	II	III	III	III	III	
Scene ->	Pro	1	2	3	4	1	2	3	4	5	1	2	3	4	Ep
Page->	1	7	17	24	31	35	41	48	52	59	63	67	71	77	82
Character															
Archie	X	X	X	X		X			X	X	X	X	X	X	X
Yuri	X	X	X	X	X		X		X	X	X	X	X	X	X
Pre		X	X	X		X	X		X	X	X	X	X		
Murgi		X	X	X		X			X	X	X	X	X	X	
Scarth		X		X			X			X*			X		
Igor		X		X			X		X	X			X		
Calypso		X*	X	X	X		X		X	X	X	X	X	X	
WOOs			X	X	X			X					X		
Mia			X								X		X	X	
Meemies				X*											
Tenty				X											
Tiger				X*									X*		
Shrooms					X										
Sam					X			X					X	X	
Draken							X*								
Fins							X								
Rolly									X	X					
Crab					X*				X*						

Giant Troll									X *				
Cab Skunk									X *				
Ivy									X *				
Gorgon										X *	X *	X *	
Furies										X *			
Moth										X			
Gryphon							X					X *	X *
Peter												X	X
Beetle													X *

- *= No Dialogue

Note: allow 1 minute per page for costume changes if multiple characters

84

APPENDIX F

The Pirate Chief's Riddle

In the seas around Sumatra, pirates lurked preying on large ships containing cargo and many passengers. One time, when a small pirate ship captured a large merchant ship, the pirate chief made an offer to the captain of the merchant ship that might save his life.

The pirate chief said he could not keep all the passengers and ordered his crew to line up all 500 of them in a straight line from the bow of the deck to the stern, and ordered his first mate to stand in the first position. He told the captain he would give him a chance to pick his own place in line after he told him what he was about to do. In a tankard were the numbers from 2 to 7. After the captain stood in line, the pirate would pick one of those numbers at random. If the number were two he would throw overboard every 2nd person and stop. But if the number were three then he would toss overboard every 3rd, and then go back and throw over every 2nd of the remaining ones. The higher the number the more times he would go through the line. If seven he would throw over every 7th, then every 6th of the remainder, then every 5th down to 2. The captain could not stand in first position and did not know which number would be picked. He stood behind the first mate and thought for a moment. Then he slowly paced off positions in line starting with the first mate until he took a place in line where he was perfectly safe no matter what number the pirate chief picked.

If you were the captain what position would you take? How many paces did he take?

85

MONTOBA – ACTORS and CHARACTERS

Actor-> Character	1	2	3	4	5	6	7	8	9	10	11	12	
Archie	X												
Yuri		X											
Pre			X										
Murgi				X									
Scarth					X								
Igor						X							
Calypso							X						
WOOs								X	X				
Mia										X			
Meemies				X	X					X	X	X	
Tenty				X	X						X		
Tiger										X		X	
Shrooms					X					X	X	X	
Sam						X							
Draken			X	X	X								
Fins								X	X	X	X	X	
Rolly								X					
Crab						X		X	X				
Giant Troll										X			
Cab Skunk												X	
Ivy										X			
Gorgon											X	X	
Furies								X	X	X			
Moth				X	X								
Gryphon											X	X	
Peter			X										
Beetle								X	X				

Note: with 12 actors there must be quick costume changes for multiple characters